The Elephant's Airplane
and Other Machines

The Elephant's Airplane
and Other Machines

Adapted from the French text written
by Anne-Marie Dalmais

Illustrated by Doris Susan Smith

A GOLDEN BOOK • NEW YORK
Western Publishing Company, Inc.
Racine, Wisconsin 53404

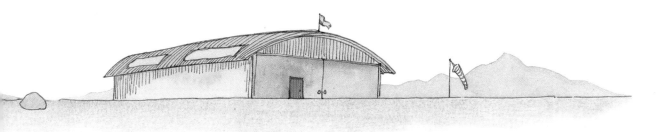

CONTENTS

Raccoon Limited, Maker of Fine Machines

Animals come from far and wide to order custom-built machines from Raccoon. He can build anything that moves -- anything a particular animal might need or fancy.

Right now Raccoon's working on a magnificent airplane for Elephant. When it's finished, Elephant will join the other proud owners of Raccoon's marvelous machines.

Snail's fondest wish came true
after a visit to Raccoon.
"This certainly beats
my old snail's pace,"
he says with a chuckle,
as he flashes by
in his rip-roaring racing car

Chicken was never happy just peck, peck, pecking around the barnyard with the other hens. Now she risks getting her feathers wet, shooting the rapids in her new kayak, specially designed by Raccoon.

Rabbit wanted to see the world,
but he needed something practical to travel in.
Raccoon obliged, and now Rabbit's exploring
a tropical forest where no other Rabbit has ever
before set paw.

Since when do cats go to sea?
Since Raccoon designed this unusual submarine.
Now Captain Cat and his crew can have fish
for supper every night.

When Antelope inherited an elegant country house from her rich old aunt, she wanted an elegant motorcar to match. Raccoon had just the thing.

Rhinoceros wanted to float gently among the clouds,
far from the roars of the crowd at the waterhole.
Raccoon's invention works perfectly,
but it's not as quiet up there
with the seagulls as Rhinoceros thought it would be.

Lizard grew up where the temperature
never fell below 90 degrees.
What did he want more than anything in the world?
To see snow, of course. But how could he keep
from catching a terrible cold?
Luckily, Raccoon had a solution.

Above the chilly mist,
Cow takes an early morning spin.
With a flick of his wing,
Hawk glides out of her way just in time.
  "Flying cows," he mutters. "What next?"

Platypus was far too slow underwater to catch
the fish he fancied. Gathering clams was a problem
because he was always short of breath.
Now, it's a different story after a helping hand from Raccoon.

Not content to wallow happily in the river,
Hippopotamus longed to race gracefully through the water.
With a little help from Raccoon,
he's now the fastest hippo around.

Ostrich always thought he should be able to fly.
"After all, I am a bird," he complained to Wildebeest.
"Perhaps you should talk with Raccoon,"
his friend suggested.
He was right.

Alligator was bored with slithering through
the muddy water. When he saw some humans buzzing around
the swamp in an odd looking machine,
Alligator went straight to Raccoon.

"Birds are supposed to fly," thought Penguin.
But unlike Ostrich, she wanted something
her friends could fly, too.
Raccoon had the answer.

The ground shakes day and night ever since
Raccoon designed a jet-powered excavator for Mole.
With all the noise, no one can get any sleep.

40

Thanks to Raccoon, Octopus is no longer confined beneath the waves. Whenever the weather is fair, he burbles up from the sea in his amphibious machine to see what's happening on the beach.

"If only I had hands and legs,"
Snake said with a sigh.
     Raccoon came up
with the next best thing.
Now Snake's
the happiest reptile around.

THE END